D1191375

BOG HOLLOW BOYS

Bog Hollow Boys is published by
Stone Arch Books, a Capstone Imprint
1710 Roe Crest Drive
North Mankato, Minnesota 56003
www.mycapstone.com

Cataloging-in-Publication Data
is available at the Library of Congress website.

ISBN: 978-1-4965-4055-3 (library bound)
ISBN: 978-1-4965-4059-1 (eBook pdf)

Summary:
Brothers Austin and Ethan Finch know their way around a body of water. But when
some of the fish start dying off and no one can figure it out, the Bog Hollow Boys
find themselves in deep water.

Designer: Ted Williams
Editor: Nate LeBoutillier

Printed and bound in Canada.
010010S17

SLEEPING WITH THE FISHES

BY C.B. JONES

STONE ARCH BOOKS
a capstone imprint

TABLE OF CONTENTS

The **BOG HOLLOW BOYS** vow

to protect, serve, and nurture the animals in and around B.H.S.P. (Bog Hollow State Park). No animal is too small, large, cute, ugly, slimy, furry, feathered, stinky, or dirty for their attention. Bog Hollow Boys to the rescue!

AUSTIN "ACE" FINCH

Age: 12
Skills: Leadership, Grit, Birds

NELLIE TIBBITS

Age: 12
Skills: Smarts, Sass, Snakes

DARYL "DA SNAKE" TATE

Age: 12
Skills: Jokes, Wrestling, Pets

ETHAN "EL GATOR" FINCH

Age: 10
Skills: Tagging Along, Wrestling, Fish

RANGER FINCH

Father of Austin and Ethan
and the warden of B.H.S.P.

DR. TIBBITS

Mother of new girl Nellie
and famous herpetologist

MS. FINCH

Mother of Austin and Ethan,
P.E. teacher, & wrestling coach

MISS DENISE

Granny of Daryl Tate, lover
of cats, & outstanding cook

THE MANLEYS

Bad boy brothers who are
always up to no good

WILLIE AND BUD

B.H.S.P. junior rangers who keep
a watchful eye on the park

CHAPTER ONE

SWAMP MONSTER

The Bog Hollow State Park Junior Bass Fishing Tournament was only a week away. Austin Finch and his little brother Ethan were out at the park checking fishing holes with their dad, Ranger Finch. None of them had sniffed a bass all day.

Ranger Finch paddled from the back of the canoe while Austin paddled up front. Ethan stuck his head over the side, looking for any swamp monsters that might want to wrestle him.

Ranger Finch sighed and scolded him again. "How many times I gotta tell you, son? When we're out in the swamp, you keep your head and arms inside the canoe at all times."

"Sorry, Daddy," Ethan said, sitting back up in the canoe. "I was just lookin' for some monsters."

"Well, no animal would want you stickin' your nose in their business like that," Ranger Finch said.

He was guiding them into the marshiest parts of Eagle Creek. He was looking for one last murky spot that might reveal a whole school of hungry bass.

"Think this is where all the bass are hidin'?" Austin asked.

Each spring, Ranger Finch organized a junior fishing tournament. The entrance fees helped keep the park open when business was slow.

Business had been especially slow that year. A frost had kept most fishers away. There'd been grumblings among the local anglers that spring. They'd been asking where all the bass had gone.

Ranger Finch guided the canoe toward a downed tree floating in the water.

"I don't know, boys. I just don't know," Ranger Finch said as he steadied them in the current. "If this keeps up much longer, we'll have to . . . "

He trailed off when he saw the way Austin was looking at him with alarm. *No reason to get him all riled up again, trying to save the world*, Ranger Finch told himself.

"Is it true?" Austin asked. "Are the locals callin' it Bassless Hollow State Park?"

"Well," Ranger Finch said, "that's what happens when nobody catches a bass for a month and a half."

Austin puffed up his chest and stuck his chin out. "They won't be sayin' that after next week," Austin said. "Not with all the big monster bass I'll be catching at the tourney."

"I'm sure you will, son," said the ranger. "But you and your brother are the only ones signed up so far."

Before Austin could say anything more, Ranger Finch turned his attention to Ethan. The youngest boy was laid out across the middle of the canoe on his stomach. His head and arms hung over the side while he skipped his lure along the surface of the water.

"Ethan!" Ranger Finch said. "If I have to tell you one more time . . ."

Before he could finish, the boat jerked and Ethan's line started squealing. Whatever it was nearly took Ethan and the rest of them along for the ride.

"The battle begins!" Ethan yelled.

When Ranger Finch saw Ethan's line go taut, he dropped his paddle and lunged for his son's legs.

"It's the big one, Daddy!" Ethan yelled back over his shoulder. "He wants to wrestle."

Austin sat there and watched the whole thing unfold. He was both jealous and in awe. *How big of a bass is that monster?* he thought.

Ranger Finch held Ethan tight and yelled at Austin "Well, don't just sit there, Austin! Start paddling."

Together they steadied the canoe and reeled in enough line for Ranger Finch to get the net down. The whole ride back to the dock, the fish flopped about in the bottom of the boat.

The fish was still clinging to the net when they got back to the dock. It was long and snake-like, and a row of small, but powerful, jagged teeth snapped shut on the line.

"That's some monster you wrestled in," Ranger Finch told his youngest son. He reached for a pair of pliers and some safety gloves.

"It really does look like a swamp monster," Austin said. Now he was even more jealous of his little brother for catching it.

"What kind of bass is that?" Ethan asked as he peered down at the still-quivering fish.

"That ain't no bass," Austin said. "Look at all those sharp teeth."

"That right there's a mudfish, boys," said Ranger Finch. "And by the looks of it, it's probably been swimmin' these waters since before this land was settled. Might also be the big old bully that's been scarin' off all our bass."

CHAPTER TWO

FROG LEGS

All told, the Finches did okay. They netted a few fliers, a couple channel cats, and one sixteen-pound, twenty-two-inch swamp monster.

They were headed over to Miss Denise's for a fish fry cookout.

"Miss Denise won't be happy with us," Ranger Finch told his sons. "I think she was lookin' for some fat bass to fry up. Not this batch of scaly mutts we snagged."

When they got Miss Denise's house, she was out back, barking out orders. "About time, Melvin," she told Ranger Finch, without looking up. "Any longer and I was about to send out your deputies here on a search party."

Ranger Finch's deputies, Bud and Willie, had left work early to get first dibs on Miss Denise's famous fried frog legs. But she'd put them to work, setting up the picnic table. Bud and Willie were doing their best to look busy and avoid eye contact with their boss.

Miss Denise grabbed Willie by the elbow the way other grandmas grab their grandkids by the cheeks. "These boys were nice enough to close up early at the park to help me get things set up."

Ranger Finch narrowed his eyes and took a good long look at his deputies. "That so?" he said. He went silent for a moment to let his deputies sweat a little. Finally he said, "Well, when they get done with that, tell 'em that they got some fish to clean inside."

Both Ethan and Austin watched Miss Denise's screen door slam shut behind their dad. It was only a matter of time before she'd turn her attention on what they could do to help out.

At the moment though, Miss Denise seemed more focused on whatever was tromping around the marshes behind her house.

She hooked her pinky fingers in her cheeks and wolf-whistled loud enough to wake up every dog in the neighborhood. "Where are all my fresh frog legs?" she hollered.

At first Austin couldn't see who or what she was yelling at. Then two mud-caked figures came marching out of the woods. One of them was holding up a pail. The other had a fishing net.

Austin let out a low groan as he saw his arch enemy, Nellie Tibbits, hold up a pail full of frogs.

"Got 'em right here, ma'am," the girl said.

Miss Denise's grandson Daryl Tate was a few steps behind. Daryl was supposed to be Austin's so-called best buddy in the world. But here he was hanging out with Nellie.

"We netted more bullfrogs than you can shake a stick at," Daryl said.

Miss Denise finally turned her attention to Austin and Ethan. "Y'all Finch boys hungry or what?"

"Yes, ma'am," they both said.

"Good," she said. "Then grab yourselves some buckets and rubber gloves. Help these two get them frog legs cleaned and prepped."

"You mean," Ethan said, "we have to take apart the frogs?"

"Where else did you think frog legs came from?" said Daryl.

Austin swallowed hard as he looked into the bucket. The bullfrogs looked up at him with their big wet eyes.

Miss Denise turned back and smiled a crooked smile at Ethan. "I don't know how you Finch boys were raised, but 'round here we work for our food. Makes it taste even better when you do it yourself." She laughed a little bit at her own joke.

Ranger Finch said, "How about I do the hard part, and you and the gang help Miss Denise clean and fry up the legs?"

When Austin turned back, Nellie smacked him in the chest with the muddy pail.

"Don't worry, Ace," Nellie said. She wiped the mud off her hands on Austin's untucked shirttail. "I'll show you how to get your hands dirty."

CHAPTER THREE

SOMETHING FISHY

Miss Denise wasn't wrong: the frog legs were especially tasty. Or perhaps the extra work had just ramped up Austin's appetite. Either way, he was starving by the time the first batch of legs came out of the fryer.

As soon as Austin sat down to eat, though, he felt something cold and slimy brush up against his foot. He jumped up out of his seat to find a white bulldog gnawing on a couple small fish heads under the table.

Austin hadn't noticed Hobie and Hunter Manley, but there they were, sitting off to the side of the garage. They were shoveling frog legs in their mouths. Just when Austin thought things couldn't get worse.

The Manley twins had been Austin's mortal enemies since preschool. Between the Manleys and Nellie, Austin suddenly lost his appetite.

"I see y'all been working with Bubba on his table manners," Austin said. He reached down with his foot and tried to kick the fish head away. But Bubba snatched it and growled at him.

"Careful, Finchy," Hunter said. "Old Bubba gets a little touchy about his fish. He near took off Daddy's hand when he tried to grab a bucket of leftover fish heads away from him."

"Who eats only the fish heads?" Nellie said. Since Nellie was a vegetarian, she was busying herself picking the ham out of her collard greens.

"Who eats only vegetables?" Austin shot back.

"Bubba sure do love him some fish heads," Hobie said. "Daddy says he's getting too fat off 'em. He says we can't keep feedin' him all them bass we—"

Hunter gave his brother a short sharp jab to the ribs. Hobie just about choked on a frog leg mid-sentence. He swallowed to clear his throat. Then he let out a belch.

What a coincidence, Austin thought to himself. Bubba had developed a taste for fish heads at the same time all the bass at Bog Hollow went missing.

"Who invited you two anyway?" Austin asked them.

As soon as he said it, the screen door slammed behind him.

"I did!" Miss Denise said. "You got a problem with being neighborly?"

Austin spun just in time to see Miss Denise coming with another fish head.

"At least these boys had the courtesy to bring me some nice bass fresh from their pond," Miss Denise said. "Instead of this!"

She slapped it down in front of Austin. He instantly recognized the mudfish's jagged teeth and snake-like face. The black eyes were now lifeless.

"You Finch boys thought I'd enjoy fryin' up some nasty trash fish for dinner?" Miss Denise asked.

"Wasn't me," Austin said, shaking his head. He pointed to Ethan.

"Wasn't me," Ethan said. He pointed at Daryl. "Daryl said you fried up the best mudfish in all of Eagle Creek."

Miss Denise picked up the fish head and pointed it at Daryl, then back at Ethan. Her face softened into a wry smile. "Y'all know well as I do Mr. Snake Boy here is the world's worst fisherman. And also, have you ever watched this boy eat? He'd suck the head off a cockroach if I put a little hot sauce on it."

Everyone burst out laughing. Everyone, that is, except Daryl.

"Well, then pass the hot sauce my way, Daryl," Ranger Finch said. "Because we're about to eat what the locals call the cockroaches of the swamp. Seems like that's all that's left at Bog Hollow."

CHAPTER FOUR

LURING IN CONTESTANTS

After dinner, everyone sat at the table and debated the merits of mudfish.

"I don't know what the big deal is," Willie said, picking his teeth. "Tastes pretty good to me."

"Yeah, sure," Bud said. "If you got Miss Denise to cook 'em. But nobody else wants them. They want bass. And as long as Bog Hollow is overrun with mudfish, there won't be no bass. And without bass, there won't be no fishermen buying fishing licenses from us."

"It does seem like the mudfish have run off the bass," Ranger Finch admitted. "But I've fished plenty of places where both bass and mudfish thrived."

He asked the Manleys how the bass were doing up at their new pond.

"They're good," Hunter said. "Just hold out your net and wait for them to jump in."

"Huh," Ranger Finch said rubbing his chin. "Where y'all stocking them from?"

"Here and there," Hobie said.

Bubba, having filled himself with fish heads, was sleeping. Hobie reached down to pat the dog's head. "Old Bubba here's developed a real nose for—"

Hunter jabbed him once again in the ribs, then cleared his throat. "Fish hatchery mostly," Hunter said. "Daddy says he's sick of fightin' off gators and snakes for every fish he pulls out of Bog Hollow. That's why he went and built the fish pond in the first place."

"Real sportin' of ya," Austin muttered. "Why don't y'all just go down to the grocery store and fish out a couple fillets at the meat cooler? That might be even easier."

"Give it a rest, Austin," Ranger Finch said. He narrowed his eyes as he watched Hunter and Hobie pick fish out of their teeth. "They ain't breaking any laws, I guess."

"Guess you're right," Austin said. "Probably why they ain't signed up for the tournament next weekend. They're scared."

"Why would we want to run around all day in the swamps tryin' to catch some nasty mudfish?" Hobie said. "We got all the bass we want right in our backyard."

"What tournament?" Nellie asked.

"The annual Bog Hollow Junior Bass Fishing Tournament," Bud said.

"Only this year we might have to drop the word *bass* since there ain't none out there," Willie said.

"Well, sign me up either way," Nellie said. "I was just thinking it's been a few weeks since I've beaten these boys at any of their own games."

"You don't even eat fish!" Austin said, his face reddening with exasperation.

"You can eat all the fish you want, Ace," Nellie said. "I'll keep the fishing trophies for myself."

Austin thought his head might explode. He was angry with Daryl for hanging out with Nellie in the first place. He was angry with Daryl's grandma for

inviting the Manleys for dinner. And he was angry with the Manleys because they were the Manleys.

Hunter sneered at Austin. "Bog Hollow is out of bass," he said. "Our daddy's got the only bass in spittin' distance of the bog."

"That's true," Ranger Finch said. He tipped back his hat and stroked his moustache. "You think your daddy would let y'all compete in our first annual Bog Hollow *Mudfishing* Tournament?"

CHAPTER FIVE

RUNNING THE NETS

That next morning, the Bog Hollow Boys were up and at 'em early. Ranger Finch said that if mudfish were taking over the bass habitats, it was time to employ some science. It was time to tag the mudfish with trackers.

"I'll meet you out at the park," Ranger Finch said. "You boys go drag Daryl out of bed and get him going."

It took Austin and Ethan a bit longer to get to Daryl's house, pedaling in their oversized hip-waders. They offered Daryl a pair, but he had no intention of going near the water.

"Nuh-uh," Daryl told them. "No way. Da Snake done told you a million times, now. Da Snake don't go swimmin'."

Ethan shook his head. "Don't swim?" he said. "Or can't?"

"Da Snake's gonna catch him some rays," Daryl said. "Maybe even a few winks."

"We're working today," said Austin. "It's not a vacation day. Now hurry up."

By the time they got out to Bog Hollow, Nellie and her mother were already there.

"About time," Nellie said, tapping her watch. "We were just about to send the search party."

Daryl wandered over to where Dr. Tibbits had set up in the pavilion. On one of the tables she'd lined up several large syringes.

"What's the plan, Dr. Tibbs?" Daryl asked. "Get rid of as many of them nasty fish as possible?"

"Just the opposite," Dr. Tibbits said. "We're tagging the mudfish." She showed him a box filled with what looked like tiny pieces of wire. Each was no bigger than a single sprinkle. "As we pull the fish out of the water, I'll use the needle to place this PIT in each fish."

"Pit?" said Ethan.

"It stands for Passive Integrated Transponder tag," said Dr. Tibbits said. "It's a tiny microchip we put in the fish. The next time we catch a mudfish, we can scan it and see if it has the chip in it. If it does, we know it's one of ours."

"Sounds like a fish barcode," said Daryl.

"It's very similar to a barcode, actually," said Dr. Tibbits. "Just like scanning groceries at the grocery store."

Nellie said, "We can even track each fish on the computer! And then use the data to learn exactly how far the mudfish are spreading. And whether or not they're taking over the old bass habitats!"

Austin muttered, "Thanks, Dr. Nellie."

"What about the bass?" Ethan asked.

"We'll tag any we find today too," said Dr. Tibbits. "I just worry we won't have many to tag."

Ranger Finch was already in the river, spreading a wide net to catch the fish. The net was so large, he needed Bud and Willie at either end. The men spoke quietly among themselves as they dragged the net upriver toward the gushing dam.

"Where do you want us?" Austin asked.

"Too dangerous in the water, boys," Ranger Finch said, barely looking up. "The current up by the dam will suck you under. Y'all help Dr. Tibbits, okay?"

Nellie grabbed the clipboard as if she were in charge. "You guys will be in charge of handing the fish off to my mom," she told Ethan and Austin.

Austin watched as Bud, Willie, and Ranger Finch wrestled the net.

"You listening, Ace?" Nellie said.

Dr. Tibbits wiped the fog off her glasses and shot her daughter a look. She grabbed a syringe and showed it to Austin. "How about this? You can help me perform the surgery," she told him.

Austin nodded, but he wasn't interested. When Dr. Tibbits turned to get the tagging station ready, Austin took off toward the water. He hitched up his waders and started to climb into them so he could help his father, but Willie grabbed him.

"Hold on there," Willie said. "Your daddy gave us strict orders to keep you young ones out of the water."

"C'mon, Willie," Austin snapped. "I'm not a baby. I can help with the net."

Willie shook his head. "No, sir."

"Well, you're not my daddy," Austin shot back. "So how about you stop acting like it and let me go!"

There was moment of silence after the words left his mouth. Austin felt everyone staring at him. He could also see his father splashing toward the bank, marching right toward him.

What scared Austin most was the calmness on his father's face. No sign of clenched teeth or knitted eyebrows.

Ranger Finch didn't even blink when he reached his son. "That's not how we talk to adults, young man." He took Austin by his shoulders and turned him to face Willie. "You apologize to Ranger Betts, now" he said.

Austin didn't dare question his dad's orders. "Yes, sir," he said. "Sorry, Willie."

"It's all right," Willie said.

Ranger Finch turned Austin to face him. "Now grab your gear and head home."

Austin felt a hot sting behind his eyes. "I said I was sorry," he said. "I want to stay and help!"

Ranger Finch looked his oldest son straight in the eyes. "You will go home right now," he said quietly, "and you won't be leaving your room again until you can speak to adults with respect."

Austin dropped his head. "Okay," he said.

The worst was the walk of shame. He almost lost his temper again while he walked past Nellie and Ethan staring at him. At least Dr. Tibbits was nice enough to busy herself and pretend nothing had happened.

Austin hopped on his bike. "I hope all y'all have a wonderful day tagging fish without me." He pedaled fast so they wouldn't see the tears in his eyes.

CHAPTER SIX

LOOKING
INTO THE SUN

Austin meant to obey his dad and head straight home. He knew this grounding was a bad one. Any detours on the way home, and he might be banned from the fishing tournament altogether by his daddy.

But on his way out of the park, he came across a few dead fish scattered along the trail. The heads had all been chewed off. The rest of the bodies had been left to rot.

"Who'd eat the fish heads and throw away the good stuff?" Austin asked. It didn't take much more investigation to give Austin an idea. There were four-wheeler tracks pressing the carcasses into the ground. Austin took one look and knew who they belonged to.

"The Manleys," he whispered.

He had to investigate what the Manleys were doing. He knew it was up to him. Even if it meant directly disobeying his dad's orders. Even if it meant that he might lose his fishing privileges for the rest of his life.

Austin ditched his bike in the woods behind the Manleys' pond. He tiptoed the last fifty yards as quietly as he could, avoiding branches and pinecones.

As soon as he had a visual on Hunter and Hobie through the trees, Austin regretted it. They were both fishing shirtless from a small boat in the middle of the pond. Their pale freckled skin was as bright as a blazing sun blinding Austin's eyes.

Austin half wished the scene *had* blinded him. He didn't care to open his eyes and see it again.

"Just don't look directly into the sun," Austin told himself.

When Austin opened his eyes again, he saw Mr. Manley heading toward the pond. He had Bubba trotting at his heels and Miss Stella the cat cradled in his arm. In the other arm, he was shaking a small headless fish.

"Y'all killin' my babies?" Mr. Manley yelled, shaking the headless fish. "We just stocked these babies a week ago, and y'all are out here fishin' them already?"

One of the twins said something back Austin couldn't make out.

But he could hear Mr. Manley yelling. Mr. Manley's low raspy voice boomed like a bullhorn from the dock. "And just how do you two geniuses think we get a pond stocked full of trophy bass? You think it's by feedin' 'em all to these two furballs?"

Whatever Hobie and Hunter were giving for excuses, Mr. Manley wasn't having it. He chucked the fish carcass into the pond.

"Y'all have got just one week," he yelled as he turned back toward the house. "Find me some more babies to replace all the fishies y'all been feedin' to these beasts."

"You gotta be kidding me," Austin said under his breath. *Is it obvious only to me that the Manleys are poaching fish?* Austin thought. *There's got to be some way to prove it.*

Hunter and Hobie bickered and reeled in their lures. On their way to the dock, the boat kept drifting toward Hobie's side. Hunter reached over and pulled up a small stringer of three baby fish Hobie had hidden under his feet.

"Are you an idiot?" Hunter said, holding up the tiny fishlings. "Daddy's gonna drown the both of us if we pull any more babies out of here. You're supposed to be throwin' the little ones back!"

Hobie's back was turned when he said whatever he said back to Hunter. But whatever it was, it made Hunter lunge to punch his brother in the shoulder.

The boat didn't stand a chance when Hunter's weight came down on Hobie's. The boat dumped both Manleys into the pond.

Hunter yelled at Hobie to help him flip the boat back over.

Hobie's voice cracked as he yelled back: "I can't, Hunter. I think something ate my shorts when I went under."

"Maybe a mudfish got 'em," Hunter said with a snicker.

"It's not funny," Hobie said. "I can't find my shorts anywhere. I'm naked!"

Austin crept back toward home. He had more than enough to worry about without being blinded by a full Manley moon.

CHAPTER SEVEN

SNAKE IN THE DARK

Austin suffered through his grounding for almost a week. But the tournament would start at dawn on Saturday. By Thursday, he decided he couldn't take any chances.

Each day that passed meant another day the Manleys were likely stealing bass from the state park. In fact, they'd probably doubled their efforts with Austin on the sidelines. There wouldn't be any fish left for the weekend's tournament.

So on Thursday night, Austin waited until he could hear his mother's snores rattling the house. Then he checked to make sure Ethan was out cold. He couldn't risk letting his little brother tag along this time.

Satisfied that he was in the clear, Austin crawled out the back window, hopped on his bike, and headed for Daryl's.

Austin tapped Daryl's window lightly. A scraggly black cat suddenly hopped on the sill and hissed. It just about sent Austin tumbling backward.

Austin started to tap again when Daryl's face popped up, wide-eyed. This time, Austin did go backward, where he fell down hard on top of his bike.

By the time Austin rolled off the bike and gathered himself, Daryl had slipped out the window in his snake pajamas.

"You crazy, Ace?" Daryl whispered. "Da Snake is not going anywhere with you like this. Da Snake is getting back in his warm bed to curl up with—"

The window clanged as the cat pawed it shut.

"Well, no excuses now," Austin said. "We might as well scoot now before your granny wakes up."

Daryl hiked up his pajama pants and crawled on the back of Austin's bike.

Out at the park, they set up camp in the old mill house above the dam. *If the Manleys are stealing bass, then they'd do it here*, Austin told himself. *The busiest fishing spot in the whole park.*

As the night turned into morning, Daryl kept falling asleep. Austin had to shake him awake.

"You've got to take this more seriously, D," he said. "We only have one more day until the tournament."

"Don't worry, Ace," Daryl said with a yawn. "You're taking this plenty serious for the both of us."

By early dawn, Austin and Daryl had both dozed off. But the ATV engines purring below them startled them awake.

Austin and Daryl hit the deck of the mill house. Through a knothole in the pine board, Austin watched the Manleys kill the engines. They had two six-gallon water coolers tied to the backs of their four-wheelers.

Bubba sat at the wheel of Hobie's ride like a sleepy getaway driver. "C'mon boy," Hobie whispered. "Get you some din-din?"

Bubba didn't move. His fat jowly head flopped to the side, and he started to snore.

"Leave 'em," Hunter whispered. "He'll just be in the way." Hunter had already lowered himself down to the water to fill half the cooler.

"But Bubba loves fish," Hobie said.

Hunter looked back at the dog, now clearly asleep.

Then he looked back at his twin. "We ain't goin' fishing for Bubba's breakfast, idiot. We're restocking Daddy's pond to replace all the fish he already ate."

Hunter very nearly filled up his waders reaching down to grab the nets they'd planted at the base of the dam. He handed Hobie one side and dragged the other one up. Even with the two of them, they strained pulling the net to the shore.

When Austin saw the full net, he growled.

"Easy, Ace," Daryl whispered. He pointed at Bubba, who'd just perked up. "Let sleeping dogs lie."

Hunter and Hobie picked through the flailing bodies as if they were panning for gold. From the looks of it, they'd netted seven different shapes and sizes of mudfish, a few channel cats, and maybe four or five small bass.

Awake now and as alert as ever, Bubba hopped down to get a closer look at the pickings.

"No bass for Bubba," Hunter said, wagging a small fish at the bulldog.

"But what about these mudfish?" Hobie asked. "Daddy don't even want mudfish. He said they eat up all the baby bass and take over everything."

"Just throw 'em in the cooler, genius," Hunter said. "They're huge. Don't you think they could come in handy for that tournament?"

"I don't get it," said Hobie.

"Just trust me," Hunter said. "I'll explain the rest of it when we got back to our pond."

Up in the mill house, Austin got it. He knew what Hunter planned to do with those fish. And he knew exactly how he would prove that the Manleys were up to no good.

CHAPTER EIGHT

TROPHIES

The good news was that Daryl and Austin never got caught sneaking out after bedtime to spy on the Manleys. As far as his parents knew, Austin had complied with his grounding.

He was allowed to go to the tournament after all. But he wasn't out of the woods quite yet. He'd be attending the tournament as the cleanup crew and would have to help Bud and Willie.

It was six in the morning. The sun was just starting to peek through the trees out at Bog Hollow. The tournament started at sunup. As soon as the sun hit the water, Ranger Finch would sound the horn.

The tournament was divided into two main categories for each two-person team. There were prizes for the biggest single mudfish or the heaviest total weight for all their catches. Or both.

Nellie and Ethan had their life jackets on and were hauling their canoe down to the dock. Austin was done up in green coveralls and putting out fresh garbage bags in all the cans around the pavilion and campsites.

"Where's Daryl at?" Nellie asked.

"Yeah, Ace," Ethan said. "I thought Da Snake would show up at least to cheer us on."

Austin shrugged as he tied off that top of a garbage bag. "Y'all know Da Snake," he said. "He's always slitherin' around somewhere."

Nellie gave Ace the hairy eyeball. "What's going on with you?"

Austin shrugged again, then grabbed another garbage bag out of his back pocket. "Don't y'all have a fishing tournament to focus on?"

"You know, Ace," she said. "It's a real bummer you're going to be taking out the trash all day." She motioned at the twenty or so junior anglers gathering in the park. "Who's going to challenge me?" she asked.

Hobie and Hunter were unloading gear from the back of their dad's truck. They'd come dressed in full camo. They'd even dressed up Bubba in a camouflage life vest.

"I know one thing for sure," Nellie said. "It won't be those two boneheads."

"I wouldn't be too sure about that," Austin said with a smirk. "From what I've heard, those Manley boys know right where to go to find fish."

By the afternoon, it didn't look like Nellie or Ethan were going to beat the Manleys. Nellie had snagged a bumper crop of catfish, fliers, jacks, and brims. But none of them counted.

Their team had hooked exactly one mudfish. It was the only fish Ethan had caught. It weighed just over seven pounds, not enough to win the prize for biggest mudfish.

But Ethan wasn't ready to give up. He grabbed one of Nellie's itty-bitty fliers before she'd thrown it back. "Now we got some bait," he'd said. "Watch the master at work."

He tied the little spiky fish to the end of his line so he could dip its fins and splash them around a few inches below the surface.

"Certainly has a unique technique, doesn't he?" said Dr. Tibbits, who'd been waiting calmly in the boat all day. She buffed her glasses.

"His technique is scaring away all the mudfish," Nellie said.

Dr. Tibbits waved her finger. "Says the girl who hasn't caught any."

"It doesn't matter," Nellie said. "We have half an hour left. I'm pretty sure one seven-pounder isn't going win it."

"You should have a little more faith in Ethan," Dr. Tibbits said. "He seems to have a real knack for catching mudfish."

"I don't know, Mom," Nellie said. She didn't even recast her line. "I think our luck might be about to run—"

Before she could finish, they were interrupted by an enormous splash and Ethan's yelling.

"Got him," Ethan shouted.

Nellie spun around in disbelief.

"A little help?" Ethan said. The fishing rod was nearly bent in two. Whatever was on the other end was huge. And fierce. The water was white with splashing.

Nellie grabbed the pole and planted her feet in the bottom of the canoe. "On my count," she said.

Together, the two of them strained to pull the creature to the surface.

Dangling from the end of the line was the biggest, ugliest mudfish Nellie had ever seen.

"Chomp, chomp!" Ethan shouted with a grin that was half pleased and half frightened.

CHAPTER NINE

EL
JEFE

Nellie and Ethan paddled their way back to the judging station. They both knew they had a keeper in the bottom of their canoe. When they heaved it into the cooler, it made a satisfying thunk.

Nellie lugged the cooler up. "Check out this beast," she said, beaming.

Even Austin tipped his cap back and let out a low whistle. "That's a beaut," he said.

"Where's Daryl?" Nellie asked. She patted the cooler. "I want to show this bad boy off."

"I haven't seen that boy all day," Ranger Finch said. "How about you?" he asked Bud and Willie.

Bud and Willie shook their heads. "He wasn't helping us," Willie said. "That's for sure."

"I wouldn't worry too much," Austin said. "He'll be here eventually."

Ethan said he hadn't seen or heard anything himself. "I've been a little busy," he said patting his monster mudfish. "I named this guy *El Jefe*," he said. "It's Spanish. It means *the boss*."

Ranger Finch checked his watch. "That's time," he said. He lifted an airhorn and let out a shrill blast. The tournament was over.

As the tournament official, Ranger Finch tried to remain impartial, but it was easy to see his face beaming with pride when he weighed El Jefe.

"Sixteen pounds, four ounces," he announced to the crowd of parents and junior anglers.

He didn't bother to hide his smile when he turned back to Austin and his two deputies. "No wonder we ain't seen bass in months," he whispered. "This thing's a regular great white."

He cleared his throat to announce the winner.

Just then the Manleys finally came bumbling out of the woods. Each was dragging a water cooler. The same coolers Austin had seen them fill with mudfish and bass at the mill house the morning before.

"Hold on," Hobie said, trying to catch his breath.

"Sorry," Hunter said. "We took a wrong turn."

"Something smells fishy," said Austin.

"Probably just our cooler full of prize-winning mudfish," said Hobie.

"Yeah," said Hunter. He giggled. "Wait til you see."

"Oh," said Austin. "I can't wait to see them. Y'all really got in right at the wire." He nearly rubbed his hands together with glee. "Go ahead and give 'em a good scan.

CHAPTER TEN

FAIR AND SQUARE

Ranger Finch and Dr. Tibbits weighed the six mudfish in the Manley's coolers. None of them were close to El Jefe's size, but together they weighed close to sixty pounds.

"These are some beautiful specimens," said the ranger. "In fact, I think I'm going to hand them over to Dr. Tibbits to take a closer look."

Hobie and Hunter exchanged a nervous glance. Nellie elbowed Austin.

"Congratulations, boys," Ranger Finch said. "I think that's the heaviest string of fish at this tournament."

"So we won the weight class?"Hobie asked.

"Oh, you won, all right," Ranger Finch said. "In fact, I want to thank y'all for helping us solve a little mystery. We've been having a dickens of a time trying to figure out what happened to all our bass."

"Mudfish ate 'em all," Hobie said.

"Well that's what I thought at first," said Ranger Finch. But then my boy Austin, here, put forth another theory."

"So what'd we win?" Hunter asked, ignoring him.

Bud was almost giddy when he came back with a manila envelope in his hands. "You guys get the big bucks," he said.

"It's the least we can do," Ranger Finch said. "I mean, y'all helped find our missing bass."

"Them ain't bass," Hunter said. "Them's mudfish."

"Oh, yeah," Ranger Finch said. "We're happy you brought those back too."

"We didn't bring nothin' back," Hunter said warily. "We fished those from out here at Bog Hollow same as everyone."

Dr. Tibbits held out a mudfish. "Take a look right here," she said, pointing to the fish. "It seems that this fish, all the fish you brought us, actually, have microchips in them."

"Just like the mudfish we tagged out here last weekend," said Nellie.

Dr. Tibbits went on. "And a quick scan of each of these fish shows that for some reason, they stopped moving around the park early yesterday morning. Right around 5:37 a.m."

"Maybe they were sleeping," said Hunter.

"I doubt that," said Ranger Finch. "In fact, the computer program shows they went on a little field trip. To your house."

Right then, Mr. Manley pulled up. And Daryl Tate was riding in the front seat. All eyes turned to them as Mr. Manley ambled stiffly over to the pavilion, clutching Daryl's arm with one meaty hand.

"Daddy," Hobie said. "Tell these people that we caught these fish fair and square."

Mr. Manley ignored him. He ignored Hunter too. He surveyed the crowd. "Does anyone here know," he boomed, "why I found this young man fishing bass in my private pond?"

Daryl squirmed out of Mr. Manley's grasp. "Da Snake was just doing a little detective field work," he said. "And guess what I found?"

"I bet you found bass," said Austin. "Bass with little microchips in their bellies."

"I thought you hated fishing," said Ethan.

"Da Snake does what the job needs him to do," Daryl said.

Nellie stepped forward.

"I get it," she said. "Those Manleys have been stocking their own pond with bass from Bog Hollow State Park. And because Bubba loves him some bass, they've had to take nearly all the fish."

Then she did something Austin was not expecting. She pointed at him. "Austin figured this out first," she said. "He solved the case!"

Ranger Finch took over. "Thanks to Hobie and Hunter for helping us solve the mystery of the declining Bog Hollow bass population," he said. "And we have a very special prize for the entire Manley family."

He opened the envelope. "It's a ticket for five hundred dollars, for poaching state wildlife. I assume Mr. Manley brought his checkbook."

"Just in time, too," Austin said. "We were really starting to get strapped for cash before you found all our missing fish."

ABOUT THE AUTHOR

C.B. Jones is a transplanted Southerner who came from the Northern Great Lakes area. When not teaching collegiate writing courses, Jones spends time writing love poems and adventure novels, feeding the dog, and setting bone-crushing picks in pick-up basketball games. Other bemusements include Civil War artifact hunting, spelunking, and checkers.

ABOUT THE ILLUSTRATOR

Chris Green is an Australian artist known for creating quirky characters. He has a strong love for bad jokes, great coffee, and all things related to beards. When he isn't illustrating for film or print, you might find him re-inventing the wheel with his 3D printer, playing with power tools in the shed, binge-watching television shows, or spending time with his lovely wife and their wonderful circle of friends.

GLOSSARY

AFFECTION — a great liking for something or someone

ANGLER — a person who fishes

ARCH NEMESIS — one who is hostile or opposes the purposes of another

COMPLY — agree to obey someone's request

FLAILING — to wave or swing wildly

FRY — to cook food in hot oil

HIP-WADERS — waterproof boots extending to the hip

JAGGED — sharp and uneven

TAUT — something that is pulled tight and straight

MUDFISH

Despite their ugly nickname, mudfish can be some of the most energetic freshwater fish you can find. In fact, there's a chance that you might have a nice tussel on your hands if you happen to hook a teal-mouthed or turquoise-finned mudfish when out fishing. The mudfish tends to put up a bigger fight than most other game fish, though, and reeling it in might not be an easy task.

The mudfish happens to be one of the oldest freshwater fish out there too. They've been around since the Jurassic era. Just look at the fish and you'll understand why. Along with the ability to live in water with little oxygen, mudfish breath by using an air-bladder. In its mouth, the mudfish has a set of sharp teeth used to protect its eggs.

MUDFISH FACTS

→ Mudfish is actually a nickname for the bowfin. Other nicknames for this fish include mud pike, dogfish, griddle, grinnel, and cypress trout.

→ Mudfish can breathe both water and air.

→ Mudfish have been on the planet since the Jurassic era—which means for about 150 million years!

→ Bowfin can be brown, silver, copper, olive, and even teal.

→ Male bowfins guard the nest of eggs and will even bite humans who get too close.

→ Humans need to eat a variety of healthy foods to get minerals and vitamins in their diet. But bowfin are able to make their own Vitamin C in their kidneys.

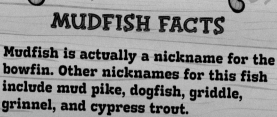

Bowfin